Goosebumps
PRESENTS

Have you seen the new show on Fox Kids TV? It's creepy. It's spooky. It's funny . . . It's GOOSEBUMPS!

Don't you love GOOSEBUMPS on TV? And if you do, then you'll love this book, *Welcome to Camp Nightmare*. It's exactly what you see on TV — complete with pages and pages of color photos right from the show! It's spook-tacular!

So check under your bed, pull your covers up tight, and start to read *Welcome to Camp Nightmare*. GOOSEBUMPS PRESENTS is so good . . . it's scary!

D0111524

Look for more books
in the GOOSEBUMPS PRESENTS series:

Episode #1 *The Girl Who Cried Monster*
Episode #2 *The Cuckoo Clock of Doom*
Episode #4 *Return of the Mummy*

Goosebumps®

PRESENTS

WELCOME TO CAMP NIGHTMARE

Adapted by Megan Stine
From the teleplay by Jeff Cohen
Based on the novel by R.L. Stine

SCHOLASTIC INC.
New York Toronto London Auckland Sydney

Adapted by Megan Stine, from the teleplay by Jeff Cohen. Based on the novel by R.L. Stine

ISBN 0-590-74588-3

12 11 10 9 8 7 6 5 4 3   6 7 8 9/9 0 1/0

Printed in the U.S.A.   40

First Scholastic printing, July 1996

WELCOME TO CAMP NIGHTMARE

1

"Here we are!" the bus driver called. He slammed on the brakes. The bus skidded to a stop.

I looked out the window. All I could see were some woods and a narrow road.

I wanted to say, "Here? There's nothing here. This isn't a summer camp."

But I didn't say any of that. No one would have heard me anyway. All the other kids on the bus were laughing and joking.

The bus driver climbed down out of the bus. Then everyone else started shoving their way off the bus, too.

We were all going to summer camp

together. Me and a bunch of other kids I had just met.

The only trouble was that I didn't see a summer camp anywhere.

My name is Billy. I'm thirteen years old. Early this morning my parents had put me on a plane to go to camp. When the plane landed, the driver of the bus was waiting for me.

He was a pudgy, older man. He had curly white hair. He wore a white cap. And a wild flowered shirt. He was waiting for other kids, too.

Finally the driver told all of us to climb on the bus. We rode for more than an hour. Then we stopped. Out in the middle of nowhere.

"Where's the camp?" I asked the bus driver when we were all outside.

He didn't answer. He just opened the storage space under the bus. He started pulling out our duffel bags.

A pretty girl with long brown hair, named Dawn, spoke up. "Where are we?" she asked.

The driver didn't answer.

"What are you doing?" a short chubby boy

named Jay asked him. Jay had brown skin and black hair. He was wearing a muscle shirt. But he didn't have any muscles to go with the shirt. "This can't be Camp Night-moon. It's the middle of nowhere!"

"Hey — Camp Nowhere!" another boy joked. His name was Roger.

"Is something wrong with the bus?" I asked the driver. "Is there anything I can help you with?"

The driver still didn't answer.

He just yanked a few more bags out of the bus and dumped them on the ground. Then he rushed back onto the bus. Before we could stop him, the driver slammed the door.

And drove off!

We jumped out of the way so the bus wouldn't hit us.

"Hey!" Mike, the youngest boy in our group, shouted. "You can't just leave us here!"

But the bus was gone. Out of sight.

I looked around at the others. Roger, Jay, Mike, Dori, Dawn, Colin . . .

3

I had learned everyone's names during the bus ride. We shrugged at each other. Nobody seemed to know what was going on.

"I can't believe the driver just took off," Dori said.

"Maybe he's crazy," Colin said. Colin was cool. He was dressed completely in black. A black bandanna on his head. Black T-shirt. Black sunglasses. He had silver chains around his neck.

"No one's ever going to find us out here," Mike cried. He sounded upset.

"Quit being such a baby," Jay snapped. He was trying to act tough. But he had a high voice. He sounded scared, too.

"Hey, keep cool, you guys," I said.

I was trying to think fast. What could we do?

But before I had an answer, I heard something.

A growl.

"What was that?" Jay cried.

I froze. I didn't know what it was. But I knew it sounded like some kind of animal.

We all held still. Something was moving through the bushes.

Then I saw it. A horrible beast — with razor-sharp teeth. And thick spiky fur. And wild, fiery eyes.

Dawn was standing right beside me.

"See that?" she whispered. She was so scared, she was almost choking.

"I see it," I said. I tried to stay calm.

"What is it?" Mike squeaked.

My heart was racing. I couldn't answer him.

"Don't run," I said quietly. "Just stay together."

I bent down slowly and picked up a rock. I pulled back and threw it at the beast.

The beast roared. Its eyes seemed to glow. Then I saw the teeth again. A horrible flash of teeth and fangs.

It lunged at us, snarling!

"Aaaaahhhh!" everyone screamed.

2

The beast backed away, still snarling. Its teeth were like small knives. They looked as if they could cut us to bits.

I didn't know what to do. I stood there, watching the growling animal.

BOOM!

Suddenly we saw an explosion in the sky. A huge bright flare burst open.

The wild beast gave a cry. Then it turned and ran into the woods.

A moment later a man walked out of the bushes. He was a big guy with a flabby belly. He had a reddish mustache and wild hair. He wore a black-and-yellow cap on his head. A whistle hung around his neck.

His yellow polo shirt said CAMP NIGHTMOON on it.

In one hand he carried a flare gun.

"This works every time," the man said to us. He pointed to his flare gun. "Shoot a flare into the sky. It scares those beasts away — at least for a while."

Then he gazed at the group of kids. He gave us a smile.

"Hi," he said. "I'm Uncle Al. I'm your camp director."

Most of us just stared at him. We were still in shock.

Finally Mike spoke up. Mike had a round face and the blondest hair I had ever seen.

"We thought we were stuck out here," Mike said.

"Sorry," Uncle Al said. He looked toward the woods where the hairy beast had run. "And sorry about *that*, too. We get a lot of wildlife up here."

"What was it?" I asked him.

"That was Sabre," Uncle Al said.

"Who's Sabre?" Jay asked.

"Sabre is not a 'who.' It's an 'it,'" Uncle Al said. He sounded pretty serious. "Just stay on the trails, and it won't bother you," he added.

Then he pointed to our duffel bags.

"Grab your stuff," he said. "We have to hike to camp. It's a mile from here. Let's go!"

Hike a mile? I thought. Great! This isn't going to be fun. Not with the heavy stuff I packed in my bag.

We all grabbed our gear. Then we started walking through the woods. The woods were thick. But the trail was wide and clear. Sunlight came through the trees. It wasn't as bad as I thought it would be.

I ended up walking beside Dawn. She was pretty. She wore a denim vest over a short cotton dress.

"Is this your first time at camp?" she asked me.

"Yeah," I said. "I usually spend the summer with relatives. My parents have to leave town all the time."

"What do they do?" Roger asked. "Rob banks?"

Then he laughed really hard. Like he thought it was soooooo funny. Dawn and I rolled our eyes.

What an idiot, I thought. Roger was always making bad jokes. He had been joking from the minute I met him in the airport.

"No, they don't rob banks," I said. "My parents are scientists. They go out on field trips a lot."

"That's a drag," Dawn said.

"It's okay," I said. "I'm used to it."

Just then we came to a fork in the path. Uncle Al blew his whistle. A young woman waiting on the path walked toward him.

"Okay, girls, listen up!" Uncle Al yelled. "This is Martha, your counselor. Go with her. Your camp is that way. It's half a mile down the path."

I waved good-bye to Dawn. She seemed really nice. Then I followed Uncle Al down the other path. We hiked through the woods some more.

Finally we came to a clearing. There were

camp buildings set in a circle around an open space.

"Boys, welcome to Camp Nightmoon," Uncle Al said.

Wow, I thought. It looks great! I saw freshly painted cabins. An office. A camp lodge. A dining hall.

Beyond the buildings I could see all kinds of sports fields. Basketball. Archery. Baseball. A lake.

"Now," Uncle Al said, "I'm going to assign you to your bunks. But first, I have a few rules. Rule number one — no leaving your bunks at night to sneak off and go somewhere."

"We'd *never* do that — would we?" Colin said. The cool one had a sneaky grin on his face.

"Rule number two," Uncle Al said. "The girls' camp is off-limits. Girls aren't part of the program."

Roger laughed. "Good," he said, smelling his arm. "Because I forgot my deodorant."

"Rule number three," Uncle Al went on.

"Lights out at nine o'clock. Wake up at six. And my last rule is the most important one. You have to write home to your parents every day. Got that? Every day."

Uncle Al smiled at us.

"Just remember," he said. "If you follow my rules, you guys are going to have the best time ever!"

"Yea!" a bunch of guys cheered.

I nodded and glanced around. Camp was going to be fun. Everything looked great — except for one thing.

On one side of the clearing, there was an old cabin. It was covered in drippy vines. A creepy old animal head was mounted on a board. It hung over the front door.

"What's that, Uncle Al?" I asked. I pointed to the rotting bunkhouse.

Uncle Al's face grew serious. "That's the Forbidden Bunk," he said quietly.

"How come it's called the Forbidden Bunk?" I asked him.

"Because it's forbidden," he snapped. "So stay away!"

After that Uncle Al led us to our cabins. I was put in a cabin with Colin, Jay, Roger, and Mike. We chose our bunks and started to unpack.

I climbed up to a top bunk. Right away I noticed the writing on the wall. Right by my pillow. The words said SABRE IS HUNGRY. They seemed to be written in dripping blood.

"Hey, who is this Sabre?" I asked the other guys.

"No one really knows," Colin answered. "But I heard he got two kids last year."

"You're kidding — right?" I asked.

Before Colin could answer, Mike let out a terrible, ear-piercing scream.

"Mike!" I cried. "What's wrong?"

I jumped off my bunk to see what was going on. Jay jumped off his, too. Mike was holding his hand and screaming in pain.

"Snake! Snake!" Jay cried. "Look! Mike got bitten by a snake!"

3

I stared at Mike's bunk bed. A huge, fat snake was lying on the sheet. It was slowly twisting itself into a knot.

The other guys went crazy. They were scared of the snake. They started running around the cabin to get away.

Think fast, I told myself. What can I do?

"Come on, guys!" I called. "Grab one end."

"Of the snake?" Colin squealed.

"No!" I yelled. "Of the sheet! We'll trap it in the sheet!"

Colin did what I asked. He picked up one end of the sheet on Mike's bed. I grabbed the other end.

"Pull up — now!" I called.

It worked. We trapped the snake in the sheet. We quickly folded the sheet in half. The snake tried to get out. But I twisted the sheet so the snake was really trapped.

Then I called to Jay. I told him to open the window. I dumped the snake and the sheet out the window.

In the cabin, Mike was still crying. It seemed like his hand really hurt.

"Get me to a doctor," he begged. "Or a nurse!"

"Just stay calm," I told him. "Hang in there, Mike."

I led Mike to the door. But before I could open it, someone pushed his way in. It was a real jerky-looking guy.

Right away I knew he must be the counselor. He was a blond teenager, about seventeen years old. He wore the same kind of yellow polo shirt that Uncle Al had on. And he had a whistle around *his* neck, too.

But this guy was skinny. Really skinny. He had big, ugly teeth. There was something awful about him. He looked as if he thought he were King of the Campers.

"Who threw the sheet out the window?" the guy demanded.

Jay pointed at me really fast. "He did it," Jay said. Then he asked the skinny guy, "You're the counselor?"

"The name's Larry," the guy said. He said it like a real geek. He even pointed at himself! Then he frowned at me. "Why did you throw a perfectly good sheet out the window?"

"There was a snake in it," I answered. "It bit Mike. We have to get him to a nurse. Or a doctor."

"Oh," Larry said. He didn't seem to care.

Mike was still moaning. He held up his hand for Larry to see. The bite mark looked awful. It was red and swollen.

"Get it away from me!" Larry said. He made a face. "I just ate! Go wash it off. Maybe I've got a bandage."

"A bandage?" I cried. "Are you kidding? This is a snake bite! We've got to get the poison out."

Larry squinted and gave me a mean look. Then he reached under his bunk bed. He pulled out a rusty old first-aid kit. He handed Mike a roll of gauze bandage.

"Mike needs to see a nurse," I said again.

"What nurse?" Larry snapped. Everything he said was in a nasty voice.

"You mean there's no nurse?" I asked. I couldn't believe it.

"No," he answered. "What do you think? Uncle Al runs a camp for wimps?"

I didn't know what to say. I couldn't believe the way our counselor was acting.

"Just wrap the baby's hand for him," Larry said. "He'll be fine." Then Larry stomped out of the cabin. He let the door bang hard as he left.

A few hours later all the campers met around a big campfire. I sat with all my bunkmates in the clearing. All except Mike. He sat by himself over near some trees. His hand still hurt. A lot.

It was a spooky night. The shadows from the fire made everybody look weird.

Uncle Al taught us the Camp Nightmoon song. It was a dumb song. It had almost no tune. It was all about how we should never whine or complain.

While everyone was singing, I brought Mike a hot dog. But he didn't feel like eating. His whole arm was swelling up. It was twice as big as normal.

"You should be in the hospital," I said to Mike.

TWEEEEEEET!

Uncle Al had stopped singing. He blew his whistle loudly and marched over to me.

"You were talking during the camp song, Billy," he scolded. "That's not allowed."

I swallowed hard. Why was he yelling at me?

"What was so important?" Uncle Al asked.

"It's Mike's arm," I said. "It's all swollen up. Mike was bitten by a snake."

"He was?" Uncle Al said. Quickly Uncle Al bent down to check Mike's hand. He pressed on his arm.

"Ow!" Mike cried.

"Good," Uncle Al said. "You've still got feeling in it. That's good."

"But it really hurts," Mike whined.

"Sure, I know," Uncle Al said. "But I've seen a lot of bites, believe me. This is nothing to worry about. The pain will be gone in the morning."

Oh, yeah? I thought. Since when do snake bites just "go away"?

"Trust me," Uncle Al said.

Then he turned and gave me a special smile.

"Guys," he called out to everyone. "I made a mistake before. I shouldn't have yelled at Billy. He was just trying to help a friend. And that's what Camp Nightmoon is all about. Billy is the Number One Camper in my book."

Everyone cheered when Uncle Al said that. But I didn't feel much better. I was still worried about Mike's arm.

The moon was really strange that night. After the campfire we walked back to our cabin. The moon was shining through the trees. There were creepy shadows on the path.

Then we passed the Forbidden Bunk. It looked like the spookiest, scariest place in the world.

Jay stopped and stared at it. He said he wanted to go in and check it out.

"You want to come with me, Billy?" Jay asked.

"I don't know," I said.

I was only half listening. I thought I heard a low growl in the woods.

"Don't tell me the Number One Camper is a chicken," Jay teased.

"I'm not a chicken," I said.

But I didn't say anything else. I was still listening.

Was there something in the woods? Was it Sabre?

As we reached our bunk, I heard the growling noise again. The bushes moved. Some kind of animal was following us. Coming closer.

The other guys filed into our cabin. I

watched the woods for a minute. Then I slipped into the cabin, too. Just as I started to close the door, I saw a shadowy beast.

It leaped onto our porch — and lunged at the door!

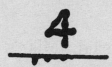

4

I slammed the door as hard as I could. Just in time.

But I still heard the beast growling. Right outside our cabin. All night long.

The next morning we woke up at dawn. We didn't have any choice. Uncle Al blew a trumpet to wake us up.

I looked out the window. The sun was just rising, and the grass was still wet. Fog rose from the ground. The camp looked unreal in the morning light.

Then I gazed around the cabin. Everyone was still in bed. Except for one person.

"Where's Mike?" I asked. "There are no blankets on his bed."

Roger made some dumb joke. It wasn't funny.

It's weird for Mike to be gone, I thought. I hopped out of bed. I opened Mike's dresser drawer and looked inside.

Empty.

"Hey, guys," I said. "Mike's stuff is gone!"

Jay peeked over the edge of his bunk bed.

"What did they do with him?" Jay asked.

All at once the other guys were worried, too. I ran outside to check.

"Mike? Mike?" I called. "Are you there?"

No answer.

Then I spotted it. The big gauze bandage that had been on Mike's hand. It was lying in the grass.

The bandage was torn — like some animal had ripped it off!

"Mike!" I called again.

No answer. Then I heard a low growling sound. Deep in the woods.

I ran back into the cabin and shut the door. Tight.

Everybody in the cabin dressed as fast as

possible. We hurried to the dining hall to see if Mike was there.

He wasn't.

I went up to the counselors' table. My cabinmates followed. Larry was already eating breakfast.

The counselors had good food on their table. They had steak, eggs, toast, and home fries. At the kids' tables, we had nothing but cold oatmeal and water.

But I wasn't thinking about food. I was thinking about Mike.

"Larry," I said to our counselor. "Mike's gone."

"Go back to your table, Billy," Larry told me. "This table is for counselors only."

"Where's Mike? Is he okay?" I asked. I wasn't going to give up. "Did Uncle Al send him home?"

"Yeah, maybe," Larry said.

"Where is he, Larry?" I repeated.

Larry stood up and gave me a mean glare. "Look, Billy," he said. "Mike's not here. So I guess he's somewhere else. Okay?"

I looked at the other guys from my bunk. They shook their heads. None of us liked Larry's answer. But somehow we knew that was the best we were going to get.

We walked back to our own table. We ate the cold oatmeal.

"Hey, man," Colin said. "Let's stay cool. I mean, Uncle Al must have sent Mike home. His hand was pretty swollen."

Yeah, I thought. Maybe.

After breakfast it was time for a game of baseball. We chose up sides.

I was on a team with Colin. Even for a baseball game, Colin wore his sunglasses and bandanna. It was a cool look.

I felt sorry for Jay and Roger. They had to play on a team with Larry — that jerk. Uncle Al was the umpire.

But the game was fun. At first. Colin got a good hit. It was a single. He ran to first base. Then I was up at bat. Roger was pitching.

I picked up the bat, but I didn't step into the batter's box. First I wanted to ask Uncle Al a question.

"Come on, Billy," Uncle Al ordered. "Batter up!"

I still didn't step up to the plate. "Uncle Al," I said. "Do you know what happened to Mike?"

Uncle Al squinted at me through the umpire's mask. "Mike? Which one's Mike?" he asked.

"Remember last night?" I said. "The one with the snake bite?"

"Oh, yeah," Uncle Al said. "The blond kid."

"Yeah," I said. "What happened to him?"

"You just play ball, son," Uncle Al said. "Don't worry about Mike. You're here to have fun. So start having it."

I shook my head. What a camp director!

Didn't *anyone* care about Mike? Wouldn't *anyone* tell me the truth?

"Step up to the plate, son," Uncle Al said in a firm voice.

I stepped up, ready to bat. But I had a funny feeling in my stomach. Roger pitched the ball, really fast. I took a swing, but I missed.

"Strike!" Uncle Al called out. He seemed happy about it.

"Come on, Billy," Colin cheered me from first base. "Hit me home!"

On the next pitch, I smacked the ball hard. Yes! A line drive to left field! The left fielder missed it. So Colin ran to second — and kept going to third.

Finally the left fielder threw the ball to Larry. Larry was the third baseman. He tried to tag Colin out. But Colin was already safe on the bag.

"You're out!" Larry yelled.

"No way!" Colin yelled back at Larry.

"Safe by a mile!" I called from second base.

Everyone looked over at Uncle Al.

"Safe at third," Uncle Al called out.

Larry threw his glove on the ground as hard as he could. "What?" he screamed.

"He was safe," Uncle Al shouted to Larry. "Now just play ball."

Larry picked up his glove. But he was still fuming. His face was bright red. He glared at

We were on our way to Camp Nightmoon, but the bus driver dropped us off in the middle of nowhere.

Then we heard a growl. Suddenly I spotted the beast. It had razor-sharp teeth and wild, fiery eyes. It lunged at us!

Uncle Al, the camp director, scared the beast away. "That was Sabre," he told us. "Just stay on the trails, and it won't bother you."

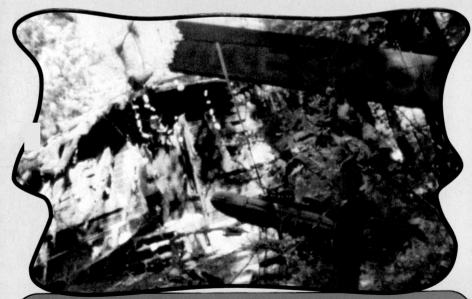

"What's that?" I asked, when we hiked into camp. "It's the Forbidden Bunk, Billy. Stay away!" Uncle Al warned.

Mike, one of the kids in my cabin, let out a terrible scream. There was a huge snake in his bed—and it bit him!

Our mean counselor, Larry, didn't even care. He said Mike would be fine.

A lot Larry knew! At the campfire that night, Mike's hand really hurt. I complained to Uncle Al, but Uncle Al said Mike didn't need a doctor.

We walked Mike back to our cabin. On the way, we saw the Forbidden Bunk. It sure looked creepy at night!

The next morning, Mike was gone. I told Larry at breakfast. But he ignored me.

That afternoon Larry threw the baseball as hard as he could at my friend Colin's head. *SMACK!* Colin fell to the ground. He didn't move for a long time.

At night we camped out in tents. Jay and Roger decided to explore the Forbidden Bunk. A second later I heard Jay scream: "Sabre got Roger!"

I had to warn Colin and Jay about this terrifying camp. But their canoe tipped, and they disappeared under the water!

I was all alone. All my friends had disappeared. I grabbed a baseball bat and went to look for help—in the Forbidden Bunk!

I met a girl named Dawn inside the Forbidden Bunk. She had run away from the girls' camp. We found hundreds of letters that had never been mailed!

Larry caught me! He grabbed my arm.

Then I saw them. "Mom? Dad? What are you doing here?" I cried. The surprises at this horrifying camp weren't over yet!

Colin — as if his eyes could burn holes into Colin's head.

Then Roger pitched to the next batter. The guy took a swing. He hit a ground ball to third — right into Larry's glove!

Colin was already running. Running toward home.

"Go on, Colin!" I yelled, staying at second. "Run!"

All of a sudden I saw a terrible look in Larry's eyes. He had the ball in his hands, ready to throw.

But he didn't throw it to the catcher.

Instead, Larry pulled his arm back in a windup. Then he threw the ball as hard as he could — right at Colin's head!

5

SMACK!

The ball hit the back of Colin's helmet. It made a horrible cracking sound.

Colin's sunglasses flew off. So did his helmet. An instant later he fell to the ground.

Then he just lay there, facedown in the dirt.

"Colin?" I cried, running toward him.

He didn't move.

"Colin?" I called again.

When I reached him, I picked up his helmet. It was lying next to his head. There was a big crack in it.

Colin still didn't move. I couldn't tell if he was okay.

Larry came running over to Colin. I figured he was going to make up some excuse. But I knew what had really happened. I saw the whole thing.

"He threw the ball right at Colin's head!" I told Uncle Al.

Right away Larry started whining. "It was Colin's fault!" Larry said with a moan. "He was running on the baseline. The ball just slipped out of my hand."

"That's okay, Larry," Uncle Al said. "Not your fault."

I couldn't believe it. Not Larry's fault? Of course it was his fault. He hurt Colin on purpose.

Then I heard Colin give a little moan. He tried to turn over. But he was still dazed. Uncle Al bent down to help him.

"What's the kid's name?" Uncle Al asked.

"Colin," I answered. "We'd better get him to a doctor."

"No, he's fine," Uncle Al said. "Come on, Colin. You're all right. Get up and walk it off."

Colin was still groggy. His face looked kind of blank. He didn't know where he was.

But Uncle Al made him stand up and walk.

"Take him to the lodge, Billy," Uncle Al told me. "Put some ice on that bump on his head. Then both of you meet us at the flagpole."

"The flagpole?" I asked. "Why?"

"That's where you're going to set up some tents," Uncle Al said. "Tonight is Survival Night. It's your cabin's turn to camp out. You sleep under the stars."

Hmm, I thought. That could be fun — at some other camp! But here? At Camp Nightmoon? I'm not sure.

Too many kids were getting hurt. And there was no nurse. And Uncle Al didn't seem to care.

Plus I wasn't sure about sleeping outside. Not with Sabre loose in the woods.

But I did what Uncle Al asked. I put some ice on Colin's head. Then I set up the tents.

By the time it was dark, I felt a little better. But Colin didn't. He was still groggy.

He and I shared a tent. Roger and Jay were in a different one.

Late that night I lay in my sleeping bag. It was after midnight. I was writing a letter home.

I told my parents all about camp. About the guys getting hurt. And about Larry being a real jerk.

Finally I turned out my flashlight.

Suddenly I heard a noise. Someone — or something — was outside my tent.

I held still — and held my breath.

"Who's there?" I wanted to say. But my voice wouldn't work. I was too scared.

In the distance I heard a moan.

All at once something burst into the tent.

"Billy!" a voice cried.

I gasped. A light blinded my eyes.

Then I saw who it was. Roger. He was shining his flashlight in my eyes. Jay was right behind him.

"Come on, Billy," Roger said. He talked in

a spooky voice. He was still trying to be funny. "Let's break some rules. The Forbidden Bunk is waiting."

I peered past Roger. The Forbidden Bunk was just across the clearing.

"You aren't really going there, are you?" I asked.

"Sure," Jay said in his high voice. "It's a perfect night."

I looked over at Colin. He was asleep. With his sunglasses on. "No, thanks," I said. "I don't think we should leave Colin. I'll stay here."

"Okay," Jay said. "Whatever."

He and Roger left. I squeezed down into my sleeping bag. Pretty soon, I drifted off to sleep.

I don't know how long I slept. All of a sudden something woke me up.

A scream. A terrible, bloodcurdling scream.

Then another one.

I sat bolt upright in the dark tent. My eyes popped open.

Then I heard a horrible, angry, animal moan. Sabre was out there — out there in the night!

"Help!" Jay called in the distance. "Somebody help me!"

I scrambled to my feet as fast as I could.

"Jay?" I cried, as I dashed out of the tent.

I ran across the dark clearing — toward the Forbidden Bunk. Then I saw a shadowy form running toward me.

I froze. My heart pounded like crazy. Who was it?

Suddenly the moonlight lit up his face. It was Jay. He looked terrified. He grabbed my arms, and I felt him shaking with fear.

"Sabre got Roger," Jay gasped. "It tore him to pieces. And it's going to get us!"

HOWWWWL!

An animal cried out in the night.

Suddenly Jay started running. He ran for his life — toward our cabin. But I didn't.

"Jay, we've got to bring Colin!" I yelled. "He's in the tent."

"Forget it," Jay called back. "We've got to get to the cabin!"

"No way," I yelled to Jay. "You do what you want. I'm going back for Colin."

I ran back toward the flagpole. I was so scared I thought I might throw up. But I had to help Colin. Finally Jay turned around and followed me.

We both stumbled toward the tent in the dark. I found it and pushed open the flaps.

"Colin! Come on!" I cried. "Get out of here!"

Colin was still groggy. He didn't move. His eyes stared straight ahead.

"Sabre is out there," Colin said. He sounded frightened — like he was having a bad dream. "Sabre is hungry."

Oh, no! I thought. He's crazy. That baseball conked him on the head and made him nuts.

"Come on, man," Jay yelled at Colin. "We have to get out of here!"

"Sabre is hungry," Colin cried out again.

I tried to think fast. What could we do? All at once I knew. I grabbed Colin's sleeping bag. I started to drag it toward the opening of the tent — with Colin in it!

"Help me," I begged Jay.

Jay grabbed the other end. Together we dragged Colin out of the tent. Then we carried him in the dark all the way across the field to our cabin. We were nearly there.

GRRRR . . .

I heard an animal growling in the woods.

GRRRR . . .

The sound came closer.

"Hurry!" I whispered loudly to Jay.

Just then Jay tripped. He fell on the ground.

"Come on!" I cried, urging him to get up. "Hurry!"

Finally Jay stumbled to his feet. He lifted his end of the sleeping bag again. We yanked and pulled and finally dragged Colin through the door of the cabin.

HOWWWL!

Sabre cried out again. The sound was so close — just outside!

I slammed the cabin door fast. There was no way to lock it. All we could do was run to the far side of the room.

"Sabre had claws," Jay said, breathing hard. "And teeth. I think it got Roger!"

HOWWWL!

"Don't let it get me!" Jay screamed in fear.

Quickly he grabbed a blanket. He hid under it. I picked up a baseball bat. I held it like a club.

GRRRR . . .

I heard scuffling noises on the porch.

Trembling, Jay and I backed up against the wall. We were both gasping for breath.

BOOM!

All at once, the door smashed open.

"No!" Jay screamed. "Here it comes!"

7

A thin, dark figure stood in the doorway. Moonlight streamed in from behind, casting a giant shadow. In the dark I couldn't see a face.

Jay and I huddled between two bunks. Jay still had the blanket wrapped around him. He shook with fear.

My heart pounded a million miles an hour.

Colin was awake. He knew there was danger and scooted his sleeping bag under a bunk.

SCRAPE. SCRAPE.

The huge figure moved into the cabin. Its monster feet dragged and scraped on the floor.

I raised the baseball bat as quietly as I could.

The monster came closer. But Jay couldn't keep quiet. He was so scared he let out a gasp.

The monster turned toward us. *Scrape. Scrape.* It walked right up to us. It reached out. Then it yanked Jay's blanket off!

"Aaaaahhhh!" Jay screamed.

A flashlight flipped on.

"What are you guys doing out of your tents?" the monster asked.

It was our counselor.

"Larry?" I said, totally surprised.

"Who did you think it was, whiner?" Larry replied.

I let out a long breath. Whew! It wasn't a monster at all.

Colin pushed out from under the bunk. But he didn't stand up. He was still too scared. He stayed in the sleeping bag on the floor.

"Close the door!" Colin cried.

"What for? Scared of mosquitoes?" Larry said with a mean laugh.

Jay and I didn't answer him. We just raced past him and slammed the door shut.

"What's your problem?" Larry asked. He sounded annoyed.

"Sabre's out there," Jay gasped.

"And it got Roger!" I added.

"Yeah," Jay said. "Up at the Forbidden Bunk. It tore Roger apart!"

"You guys went to the Forbidden Bunk?" Larry yelled. He shook his head. "That's totally against the rules!"

Who cared about the rules now? All that mattered was Roger.

"Sabre got Roger!" I repeated. "Don't you see?"

"I saw it," Jay chimed in. "I was screaming. Maybe Roger is still in the Forbidden Bunk right now. Maybe he's rotting! Maybe Mike is there, too!"

"Shut up," Larry told Jay flatly.

"What?" I said. I stared at him with my eyes wide.

"That's a real sick joke," Larry said. "Save it for the talent show."

"You don't believe us?" I asked, my mouth hanging open.

"First off, you shouldn't have left your tents," Larry said. "Second, you shouldn't have gone to the Forbidden Bunk. Wait till I tell Uncle Al. He's going to be really mad."

Then he turned and marched out the door.

For a minute I was too stunned to speak.

"I can't believe he thinks we're lying," I finally said.

"What do we do now?" Jay asked.

I thought for a moment. I heard a growl outside. "We're staying right here for the rest of the night," I said firmly. "We'll take turns guarding the door."

Jay was so tired he could hardly move. And Colin's head still hurt from the baseball game. So I offered to stay awake. I sat on the floor with my back to the door. Somehow I kept my eyes open. The other guys slept.

Finally it was dawn. I had stayed up all night. But I didn't care. All I wanted to do was find Uncle Al. I wanted to tell him about Roger being attacked.

Jay and Colin woke up. We opened the cabin door carefully and looked out. Was Sabre out there?

The coast was clear. So we made a run for it. The three of us ran the whole way to the dining hall.

The dining hall was already buzzing with kids and counselors. Uncle Al was nowhere in sight. Larry and the other counselors were eating big breakfasts again.

"Where's Uncle Al?" I asked Larry.

"Why? You got something to say?" Larry answered. "Say it to me."

"No way," I said. "You don't believe us about Roger."

"I don't even *know* anyone named Roger," Larry replied.

Huh? I thought. Roger was on your baseball team yesterday. How can you not know him?

"Look, Larry," I shouted. "I just want to talk to Uncle Al, okay?"

Larry stood up and put his face right in front of mine.

"Uncle Al's not here!" he shouted back.

"And I'm in charge. You got that? Now all you guys get into your bathing suits. You're going to the lake."

For a minute I just glared at Larry. But what for? He wasn't going to budge. So I left with Jay and Colin. We went back to the cabin and changed into our bathing suits. Then we headed down the path.

But I wasn't going to the lake. I had another plan. I wanted to call my parents. I wanted to get out of there.

Camp Nightmoon was turning into Camp Nightmare.

I turned off onto a different path.

"Where are you going?" Jay asked.

"Never mind," I said. "I'll see you guys later."

The path I took led to a pay phone. I had seen the phone before. It was mounted on a tree in the woods.

I began to run toward the tree — and the phone.

Please let my parents be home, I thought. *Please*.

43

8

I grabbed the phone fast. But the receiver felt funny. It wasn't as heavy as a real phone.

Suddenly a large hand touched my shoulder. It clamped down hard.

I gasped and spun around in surprise.

"Uncle Al!" I cried out when I saw who it was.

Uncle Al glared at me.

"What are you *doing*, Billy?" he asked in an angry voice.

"I . . . I was trying to make a call," I said, trembling.

"To your parents?" Uncle Al asked. He was still frowning.

"Yes," I admitted. "Just to say hi."

"Ha!" Uncle Al shouted, letting out a big laugh. He pointed at the phone. "Well, that thing won't help you, will it? It's a fake. I put it in as a joke."

A joke? I thought. What kind of joke is that?

"Where can I find a real phone?" I asked.

"There is no real phone," Uncle Al said. "We're too far away from everything. They won't put in a phone line up here."

I swallowed hard. No phone? Now I knew I was *really* stuck.

Uncle Al must have seen the worried look on my face. He began trying to cheer me up. He told me to keep writing letters to my parents. He asked where I was supposed to be, and I told him the lake. Then he said I should go to the lake and have some fun.

But I wasn't ready to go.

"Uncle Al?" I asked. "Did Larry ask you about Roger?"

"Yes," Uncle Al said. "I checked the files.

We don't have a camper here named Roger. No first name. No middle name. No last name." Uncle Al started to walk away.

"But that's not possible!" I called after him.

He whirled around. He glared at me with angry, fiery eyes. "Get to the lake, Billy!" he yelled.

Then he stomped off through the bushes and disappeared.

I just stood there for a minute. My head was spinning. I didn't know what to think.

No one named Roger? That wasn't true. Roger had been there yesterday, telling jokes. He couldn't just disappear.

I wanted to tell Jay and Colin about this. So I hurried down the path toward the lake.

When I got there, the two of them were already in the water, paddling a canoe. The boat was already far away from the shore.

I ran onto the dock and stood at the end of it.

"Guys!" I called. "Uncle Al says there's no Roger!"

"What?" Colin called.

I started to shout again. But a loud whistle

drowned out my voice. It was Larry. He ran onto the dock. He was blowing his whistle for Jay and Colin to come back in.

"Get back in here, you guys!" Larry shouted. "You have to put life jackets on!"

Colin and Jay started paddling back to the dock. Larry turned and handed me an old, torn life jacket. It was way too small.

"This won't fit," I said.

"Tie it on somehow," Larry answered. "Tie it around your waist."

Then he picked up two more life preservers. He tossed them off the dock toward Jay and Colin.

"Put these on!" Larry called.

Jay and Colin stood up in the canoe. They reached out to catch the life preservers. But they missed — and the canoe tipped over.

Jay and Colin fell into the water with a splash.

"You guys are hopeless," Larry called to them.

Colin splashed around, trying to swim to the dock.

"I'm not a good swimmer," he said, spitting out water.

"You don't have to be, you jerk," Larry answered. "The life preserver will keep you up."

But Colin couldn't reach the life preserver. His arms flailed around. "Help!" he cried.

"He's faking," Larry said.

No, he's not, I thought. I hurried to the edge of the dock.

"Hold on to the canoe, Colin!" I called.

Colin reached for the canoe. But the boat was upside down. And it was drifting away. He couldn't grab it.

In the next instant Colin went under.

"I'll get him," Jay called.

Jay dove under the water to find Colin. I waited. But Jay didn't come back up either.

Oh, no, I thought. My heart was pounding. Jay and Colin are both drowning!

"I'm going in!" I cried. I started to jump in the water. But Larry held me back.

"Are you nuts?" he cried. "You'll go under, too!"

"Let go of me!" I screamed.

"No!" Larry yelled back.

I fought with Larry, trying to get free. But he wouldn't let go. Before I knew it, I fell off the edge of the dock.

Then I was in the lake. I treaded water and looked up at the dock.

Larry backed away, staring at the water. His eyes were wide. His face was white with fear.

"I never saw this," he said. "I was never here." He kept shaking his head. "I didn't see any of this. It isn't my fault."

Then he turned and ran back into the woods.

"Larry!" I yelled from the water. "You can't just leave us here!"

9

I was in the water all alone. Larry was gone.

The lake felt cold. So I treaded water for a few more seconds to get used to it. Then I took a deep breath. I ducked under the surface and swam around.

Yuck. The water was murky brown. But I could see just enough. Jay and Colin were not there.

I came up for air. Just a quick gulp. Then I dove under again.

Nothing. I swam around underwater a long time. I looked everywhere. No Colin. No Jay.

Finally I couldn't hold my breath any longer. I popped to the surface, gasping.

After that I ducked under two or three more times. But I didn't find Colin or Jay.

"Help!" I cried when I swam to the surface the last time. "Larry! Uncle Al! HELP!"

No one answered my cries for help. All I heard were a few birds chirping. Then silence.

I began to shiver. The lake was so cold I couldn't stay in the water any longer. I had to climb out.

Shaking, I pulled myself onto the dock. Then I turned around and scanned the surface of the water.

Nothing. Not even a ripple.

"Jay! Colin!" I called one last time.

No one answered me.

Finally I ran through the woods, dripping wet. The stony path hurt my feet. But I didn't stop running. I didn't dare.

There was something moving through the bushes as I ran. Something that growled. I knew it must be Sabre.

I dashed away from the growl and finally

reached the camp. By then I was wheezing from running so much. My side hurt, too.

I burst into the clearing and called for help.

"Somebody! Help me!" I shouted.

Silence.

Wow, what's going on? I wondered. I looked around. The camp was empty. There was no one in the clearing. No one on the baseball field. No one in any of the cabins. No one in the lodge.

It was as if all the campers and counselors had vanished into thin air!

I ran to my cabin — cabin #4. Empty!

Even the sheets on the bunk beds were gone! All the sheets except mine.

I yanked open the dresser drawers. Empty!

All except my drawers. My clothes were still there.

"What's going on?" I cried. My lip started to tremble.

I sat down on a lower bunk. Then I curled up on the mattress. More than anything in the world, I wanted to go to sleep.

No. I couldn't let myself do it.

Get up! I told myself. I sat up and tried to be brave.

Think! I told myself.

There was only one thing to do. Change out of my wet clothes — and then go look for help.

I quickly put on a dry T-shirt and jeans. Then I grabbed a baseball bat and a flashlight. I dashed out of the cabin.

The wind was beginning to blow wildly. I looked at the gray, cloudy sky. A storm was coming.

Think! I shouted at myself. I ran toward the lodge. Still no one in sight.

Then I noticed a piece of paper on the ground. I picked it up. Weird. It was a letter from Mike — to his parents.

Why didn't this letter get mailed? I wondered.

Then I saw more of them. More letters. They were scattered all over the path — a path leading right up to the Forbidden Bunk!

Suddenly I remembered what Jay had said. Maybe Roger and Mike were in the

Forbidden Bunk. Maybe their bodies were rotting right now!

I had to find out if it was true.

Slowly I walked up to the strange, broken-down old cabin. The wind was blowing hard. I pushed the door open. It squeaked on rusty hinges.

My legs felt wobbly as I stepped inside the cabin. And I couldn't see much. It was too dark inside.

Do you really want to do this, Billy? I asked myself.

But I didn't have any choice. I had to know the truth.

I flipped on my flashlight.

YIKES! A rat ran across the floor — right past my feet.

I gasped and jumped back.

Suddenly the door closed behind me. I was trapped.

I sucked in my breath. I heard a creak. The sound of a floorboard.

There was someone else in the dark cabin — someone right behind me!

10

Don't run, I told myself.

A person was standing in the shadows behind me. I turned around slowly. All at once the person lurched forward.

"Aaaaahhhh!" I cried. I dodged out of the way and started to raise my baseball bat to protect myself.

At that moment my flashlight fell across her face.

"Dawn?" I cried in surprise. It was the girl I had met on the first day of camp.

"Billy?" she said. She was just as surprised as I was.

I shined my light at her. She was all scratched up and dirty. She looked like she'd been running through thorny bushes.

There was fear in her eyes.

"What are you doing here?" she asked.

"I'm trying to escape," I said softly.

"Really?" she said.

I nodded. "Nightmoon's a nightmare," I said.

"I know," Dawn agreed. "It's evil. I ran away, too."

"Guys are dropping like flies at my camp," I told her. "Snake bites, creature attacks, drownings . . ."

"It's the same thing at the girls' camp," Dawn said.

I shook my head. I couldn't believe it. She seemed like the only other person who knew the truth.

Then I took a quick look around the Forbidden Bunk. It was creepy inside. Hanging from the rafters were strands of rope. They dangled in my face. The place was like a haunted house.

"Hey, what's that?" I asked. I pointed to a

big trash can in the corner. It was covered with a dirty old cloth.

What is in there? I wondered. Something horrible? Maybe I don't want to know.

Together, Dawn and I walked over to the trash can. We lifted the cloth from the top. I gasped.

Letters! The trash can was filled with letters. All the letters the campers had written home.

I reached inside and pulled out a handful.

"Hey!" I said. I held up one of the letters. "I wrote this on the first day of camp."

"Yeah," Dawn said. "And some of them are from *years* ago!"

My heart started pounding. Why hadn't the letters been mailed?

"We've got to get out of here," I said. I felt panicky.

"We'll escape together, okay?" Dawn said.

I was just about to agree. But we both heard a shrill whistle. I peeked out the broken window of the Forbidden Bunk. I saw campers and counselors. They had all come back. They were doing something around the campfire.

"They were gone. Now they're back," I whispered to Dawn. "But I don't know what's going on."

"Maybe they're looking for you," Dawn said. "Or for me."

She shivered when she said that. She was really scared.

"Do you think so?" I whispered.

Dawn nodded. "I don't want them to find me, Billy," she said.

"Okay," I said. "I'd better go out and see what's happening. I'll come back here later, after lights out."

"Come back soon, Billy," she begged me. I could hear her voice shaking with fear.

"I will," I said. "I promise. I will."

I took a deep breath. Then I sneaked out of the cabin and into the clearing.

Uncle Al stood in the middle of the crowd.

He was wearing army clothes and dark sunglasses. The counselors were all wearing army clothes, too.

"Line up! Two rows! Hustle up!" Uncle Al yelled at the kids. He sounded like it was important.

I hid behind a tree, watching. But Larry, the counselor, spotted me.

"Hey, Uncle Al," Larry called. "Billy's here."

Uncle Al stared in my direction. I knew he was squinting at me from behind those sunglasses.

"Where have you been, Billy?" Uncle Al called to me in a cold voice.

I marched right up to him.

"I've been at the lake," I told him. "Where Colin and Jay drowned! And Larry did nothing to help!"

"Get in line, Billy," Uncle Al yelled at me. "We'll talk about it later."

I didn't move. Why should I? But Uncle Al waved at Larry to come over. Larry grabbed me. He shoved me into a line. I tried to get away from him. But he held on. He was too strong.

Then Uncle Al motioned to another guy. A counselor. The guy picked up two bags of equipment. He dumped them out onto the ground. Two dozen small weapons fell out.

Crossbows!

"Hand them out," Uncle Al told the counselor. "One weapon for each boy."

The counselors started passing out the crossbows.

"What's going on?" I asked.

"We have a runaway from the girls' camp," Uncle Al said. "We think she's close by. Maybe in the woods. Maybe even closer. Look everywhere. We don't want her to get away."

"What?" I shouted. Was he kidding? My mouth fell open. I got out of line and walked back over to Uncle Al. "Are you saying we should *shoot* her?"

"That's right, Billy," Uncle Al replied. "She broke the rules."

"But this is crazy!" I screamed. "You can't go around killing people!"

"Killing? Who said anything about killing?" Uncle Al replied. "These weapons are loaded with special darts. They won't kill her. They'll just stop her. They'll make her go to sleep. Have you got a problem with that?"

I raised my crossbow to my shoulder. I pointed it right at Uncle Al.

"I won't do it," I said.

"Billy," Uncle Al said. "This is no way for you to act. You're our Number One Camper."

"Camp is over, " I replied. "Nobody else is going to die."

"Die? Nobody's died here," Uncle Al said.

"You're a liar!" I yelled at him. "What about Mike's snake bite? And Sabre attacking Roger? And Jay and Colin drowning . . . "

"Mike?" Uncle Al asked. "Jay? Colin? We don't have campers here by those names."

"Liar!" I shouted again.

"Calm down, Billy," Uncle Al said. He turned to Larry. "Larry, do you know any kids by those names?"

"Nope," Larry said. "Never heard of them."

"Billy, you're just homesick," Uncle Al told me. "You're imagining things. Now put down that crossbow. Or you're going to be very, very sorry."

"No, I'm not!" I yelled.

Suddenly everyone closed in on me. All the kids came at me. And Uncle Al. He grabbed for my arms.

"No!" I cried out. I didn't have any choice. I pointed the crossbow right at Uncle Al's chest.

Then I fired!

11

POP.

The sound from the crossbow was silly. It was just a little popping sound.

A small rubber arrow shot out. A toy arrow. It hit Uncle Al in the chest — and bounced off.

What's going on? I thought. That isn't a real dart.

Then a big smile spread across Uncle Al's face. He let out a happy, whooping cheer.

"Congratulations, Billy!" he shouted. "You passed!" Then he turned to everyone else in the crowd. "He passed!"

Everyone started cheering and clapping.

Even Larry. He ran up to me with a big, happy smile on his face. He shook my hand.

"Way to go, Billy," Larry said. "You did great!"

Huh? I did great at what?

Uncle Al turned to the woods. He cupped his hands to his mouth and called, "You can come out now. Billy passed!"

Who is he calling to? I wondered. Then I saw them.

It was my parents! They came walking out of the woods. They had big smiles on their faces, too.

I ran up to them. "Mom? Dad? What are you guys doing here?" I asked.

My mom reached out and gave me a big hug. "I knew you would pass, sweetheart," she said.

Then Dawn hurried out of the woods. "Congratulations, Billy," she said, running over to me.

I blinked and shook my head. I thought I was going nuts. "What are you all talking about?" I asked.

"Billy, this isn't a summer camp," Uncle Al explained. "It's a government testing lab. And you just passed some very hard tests."

"Huh?" I said. "What about all those accidents? What about Jay and Colin?"

As soon as I said their names, Jay and Colin ran out of the woods.

"We hid under the canoe the whole time," Jay said.

"In an air pocket," Colin explained.

"But thanks for trying to save us," Jay added.

"What about Mike's snake bite?" I asked.

At that moment Mike popped up behind me. He plopped a rubber snake on my head.

"It was a fake," he said, smiling.

A minute later Roger strolled out of the woods. He was fine. Sabre hadn't eaten him at all!

I couldn't believe it! It had all been a trick! But I still didn't understand why.

"Listen, Billy," my mom explained. "Your father and I are going to lead an important scientific trip. To a very dangerous place. We wanted to take you with us. But government rules said you couldn't come along. Not unless you passed certain tests."

"What tests?" I blurted out.

"Tests for quick thinking," Uncle Al said. "Like the way you trapped that snake. And for courage. The way you went out in the night with Sabre on the loose. To help your friends."

"And trying to save Colin and me from drowning," Jay added.

"That took a lot of courage," Larry said.

"And believing in yourself," Dawn added. "Even when everyone said you were crazy."

"You knew when to follow the rules," Uncle Al said. "And when to break them."

My head was spinning. "So all of you were in on it?" I asked.

"Right. We're all actors," Larry said. "We work at this government lab."

"You were amazing," I said. "So amazing that I'll never set foot in a summer camp again!"

I thought everyone would laugh at my joke. But they didn't. They were all staring at something. Something in the bushes.

GRRRRRR . . .

It had to be Sabre!

Everyone stepped back.

GRRRRRR . . . It growled again. But this time it sounded like a roar!

Then the creature burst through the bushes. Its eyes were fiery red. Its terrible jaws were huge.

And it came straight for me!

I tried to back away, but I tripped. Almost at once the beast was on me.

GRRRRRRRRR! I closed my eyes in terror.

Then everyone started laughing.

"Say hello to Sabre," one of the counselors said.

I opened my eyes and let out a huge sigh. It was only a mechanical beast — not a real one!

The counselor who operated the beast

showed me his remote control. It made Sabre's eyes glow. A growling sound came out of a speaker in his mouth.

"Oh, man," I said, shaking my head. "I thought I was dead meat."

Everyone laughed again. The counselors gave each other high fives.

"You'd better get your things packed," my dad said to me. "We leave first thing in the morning."

"Where are we going?" I asked my mom.

"Very far away," she said. "To a place called Earth."

"Earth?" I said. "Never heard of it."

"It's right there," Uncle Al said, pointing up at the sky.

"Yes," my dad said. "And we hear that the aliens there are pretty dangerous."

"They couldn't be as crazy as Larry and Uncle Al!" I said with a little laugh.

Dad put his arm around me. Together we looked up into space. "You never know, Billy," he said. "You never know."

GET Goosebumps®
by R.L. Stine

☐ BAB45365-3	#1	Welcome to Dead House	$3.99
☐ BAB45366-1	#2	Stay Out of the Basement	$3.99
☐ BAB45367-X	#3	Monster Blood	$3.99
☐ BAB45368-8	#4	Say Cheese and Die!	$3.99
☐ BAB45369-6	#5	The Curse of the Mummy's Tomb	$3.99
☐ BAB49445-7	#10	The Ghost Next Door	$3.99
☐ BAB49450-3	#15	You Can't Scare Me!	$3.99
☐ BAB47742-0	#20	The Scarecrow Walks at Midnight	$3.99
☐ BAB47743-9	#21	Go Eat Worms!	$3.99
☐ BAB47744-7	#22	Ghost Beach	$3.99
☐ BAB47745-5	#23	Return of the Mummy	$3.99
☐ BAB48354-4	#24	Phantom of the Auditorium	$3.99
☐ BAB48355-2	#25	Attack of the Mutant	$3.99
☐ BAB48350-1	#26	My Hairiest Adventure	$3.99
☐ BAB48351-X	#27	A Night in Terror Tower	$3.99
☐ BAB48352-8	#28	The Cuckoo Clock of Doom	$3.99
☐ BAB48347-1	#29	Monster Blood III	$3.99
☐ BAB48348-X	#30	It Came from Beneath the Sink	$3.99
☐ BAB48349-8	#31	The Night of the Living Dummy II	$3.99
☐ BAB48344-7	#32	The Barking Ghost	$3.99
☐ BAB48345-5	#33	The Horror at Camp Jellyjam	$3.99
☐ BAB48346-3	#34	Revenge of the Lawn Gnomes	$3.99
☐ BAB48340-4	#35	A Shocker on Shock Street	$3.99
☐ BAB56873-6	#36	The Haunted Mask II	$3.99
☐ BAB56874-4	#37	The Headless Ghost	$3.99
☐ BAB56875-2	#38	The Abominable Snowman of Pasadena	$3.99
☐ BAB56876-0	#39	How I Got My Shrunken Head	$3.99
☐ BAB56877-9	#40	Night of the Living Dummy III	$3.99
☐ BAB56878-7	#41	Bad Hare Day	$3.99
☐ BAB56879-5	#42	Egg Monsters from Mars	$3.99
☐ BAB56880-9	#43	The Beast from the East	$3.99
☐ BAB56881-7	#44	Say Cheese and Die—Again!	$3.99
☐ BAB56882-5	#45	Ghost Camp	$3.99
☐ BAB74586-7		Goosebumps Presents #1 The Girl Who Cried Monster	$3.99
☐ BAB74587-5		Goosebumps Presents #2 The Cuckoo Clock of Doom	$3.99

☐ BAB74588-3	**Goosebumps Presents #3** **Welcome to Camp Nightmare**	$3.99
☐ BAB56644-X	**Goosebumps 1996 Calendar**	$9.95
☐ BAB62836-4	**Tales to Give You Goosebumps** **Book & Light Set Special Edition #1**	$11.95
☐ BAB26603-9	**More Tales to Give You Goosebumps** **Book & Light Set Special Edition #2**	$11.95
☐ BAB74150-4	**Even More Tales to Give You Goosebumps** **Book and Boxer Shorts Pack Special Edition #3**	$14.99
☐ BAB55323-2	**Give Yourself Goosebumps Book #1:** **Escape from the Carnival of Horrors**	$3.99
☐ BAB56645-8	**Give Yourself Goosebumps Book #2:** **Tick Tock, You're Dead**	$3.99
☐ BAB56646-6	**Give Yourself Goosebumps Book #3:** **Trapped in Bat Wing Hall**	$3.99
☐ BAB67318-1	**Give Yourself Goosebumps Book #4:** **The Deadly Experiments of Dr. Eeek**	$3.99
☐ BAB67319-X	**Give Yourself Goosebumps Book #5:** **Night in Werewolf Woods**	$3.99
☐ BAB67320-3	**Give Yourself Goosebumps #6:** **Beware of the Purple Peanut Butter**	$3.99
☐ BAB53770-9	**The Goosebumps Monster Blood Pack**	$11.95
☐ BAB50995-0	**The Goosebumps Monster Edition #1**	$12.95
☐ BAB60265-9	**Goosebumps Official Collector's Caps** **Collecting Kit**	$5.99
☐ BAB73906-9	**Goosebumps Postcard Book**	$7.95

Scare me, thrill me, mail me GOOSEBUMPS now!

Available wherever you buy books, or use this order form. Scholastic Inc., P.O. Box 7502,
2931 East McCarty Street, Jefferson City, MO 65102

Please send me the books I have checked above. I am enclosing $_____ (please add
$2.00 to cover shipping and handling). Send check or money order — no cash or C.O.D.s please.

Name _____Age _____

Address _____

City _____State/Zip _____

Please allow four to six weeks for delivery. Offer good in the U.S. only. Sorry, mail orders are not available to
residents of Canada. Prices subject to change.

GB1295

Home alone... with a monster?

Goosebumps®

Gretchen and Clark hate staying
at their grandparents' house.
Grandpa Eddie is deaf, Grandma Rose
is obsessed with baking, and they live
in the middle of a swamp!
And that's just the beginning.
There's something weird about that locked
room upstairs. The one with the strange
growling noises coming from it....

How to Kill a Monster
Goosebumps #46
by R.L. Stine

Appearing soon at a bookstore near you.